The Little Red Hen

Dona Herweck Rice

Editorial Director
Dona Herweck Rice

Assistant Editors
Leslie Huber, M.A.
Katie Das

Editor-in-Chief
Sharon Coan, M.S.Ed.

Editorial Manager
Gisela Lee, M.A.

Creative Director
Lee Aucoin

Illustration Manager/Designer
Timothy J. Bradley

Illustrator
Chad Thompson

Publisher
Rachelle Cracchiolo, M.S.Ed.

Teacher Created Materials
5301 Oceanus Drive
Huntington Beach, CA 92649-1030
http://www.tcmpub.com
ISBN 978-1-4333-0165-0
© 2008 Teacher Created Materials, Inc.

The Little Red Hen

Story Summary

Little Red Hen lives on a farm. She works hard every day. She lays eggs and takes care of her chicks. Some other animals on the farm are lazy. They do not work hard like Little Red Hen does.

One day, Little Red Hen finds a grain of wheat. She wants to plant it. But no one will help her. She plants it herself. Then she waters the plant. She cuts it when it grows. She picks the wheat and takes it to the mill. Then she bakes some bread. Still, no one helps her. Do you think the other animals will help her eat the bread? Read the story to find out.

Tips for Performing Reader's Theater

Adapted from Aaron Shepard

- Don't let your script hide your face. If you can't see the audience, your script is too high.

- Look up often when you speak. Don't just look at your script.

- Talk slowly so the audience knows what you are saying.

- Talk loudly so everyone can hear you.

- Talk with feelings. If the character is sad, let your voice be sad. If the character is surprised, let your voice be surprised.

- Stand up straight. Keep your hands and feet still.

- Remember that even when you are not talking, you are still your character.

- Narrator, be sure to give the characters enough time for their lines.

Tips for Performing
Reader's Theater *(cont.)*

- If the audience laughs, wait for them to stop before you speak again.

- If someone in the audience talks, don't pay attention.

- If someone walks into the room, don't pay attention.

- If you make a mistake, pretend it was right.

- If you drop something, try to leave it where it is until the audience is looking somewhere else.

- If a reader forgets to read his or her part, see if you can read the part instead, make something up, or just skip over it. Don't whisper to the reader!

- If a reader falls down during the performance, pretend it didn't happen.

The Little Red Hen

Characters

Narrator	Cat
Little Red Hen	Mouse
Dog	Goose

Setting

This reader's theater takes place on a farm. The farm is a busy place. Plants grow there. Animals live there. Little Red Hen lives and works on the farm.

Act 1

Narrator: The sun rises over the farm. Little Red Hen wakes up. She yawns. Then she stretches her wings.

Little Red Hen: Cluck, cluck. Oh, what a pretty day! But I must get busy. I have many things to do.

Dog: Woof! Pipe down! I am sleeping.

Cat: Meow! Me, too, silly hen.

Mouse: Squeak! Go back to sleep!

Goose: I am so tired. Yaaaaawn! Honk!

Narrator: Dog, Cat, Mouse, and Goose are lazy. They want to sleep. But Little Red Hen knows there is work to do. She is ready to get busy.

Little Red Hen: You are so lazy! Who will work if you sleep?

Dog: Not I! Zzzz.

Cat: Not I! Zzzz.

Mouse: Not I! Oh no, not I. Zzzz.

Goose: Not I! Now go away and do not bother me. Zzzz.

Little Red Hen: I will work. The farmer counts on me to do a good job. It is time to get busy.

Narrator: Little Red Hen gets to work. She gathers her chicks and feeds them. She sits on her eggs to keep them warm. She cleans the chicken coop. She is a very busy little hen.

Poem: I Had a Little Hen

Little Red Hen: My, oh, my. What a busy day! I think I will rest for a bit.

Narrator: The tired hen finds some hay. She sits on it to rest. Just then, something small catches her eye.

Little Red Hen: What in the world is that? It is a tiny grain. It is a grain of wheat!

Narrator: Little Red Hen is happy to find the grain. She likes to grow things. She knows the grain will grow into wheat. And wheat can be made into bread. Her chicks like bread.

Little Red Hen: Look what I found! It is a grain of wheat. I will plant the grain. It will grow. Then I can make bread. But I am so tired. Who will help me plant the grain?

Dog: Not I! Dogs do not plant. Dogs wag and sleep.

Cat: Not I! Cats do not plant. Cats purr and sleep.

Mouse: Not I! Mice do not plant. Mice nibble and sleep. Then we nibble some more.

Goose: Not I! Geese do not plant. Geese honk and sleep. Now go away and do not bother me. Honk!

Little Red Hen: Then I will do it myself.

Narrator: And she does.

Act 2

Narrator: Many days pass. The grain of wheat grows and grows.

Dog: How about that?

Cat: It looks like the wheat grew.

Mouse: Maybe I can have a nibble. Maybe I can have two or three nibbles!

Goose: No! Wait for Little Red Hen to make bread. Then we can all eat it. Yummy!

Little Red Hen: You must help if you want to eat. Who will help me cut the wheat?

Dog: Not I! Dogs do not cut. Dogs bark and play. Woof!

Cat: Not I! Cats do not cut. Cats meow and play. Meow!

Mouse: Not I! Mice do not cut. Mice nest and play. We nibble, too. Remember? Squeak, squeak!

Goose: Not I! Geese do not cut. Geese fly and play. Now go away and do not bother me. Honk, honk, honk!

Little Red Hen: Then I will do it myself.

Narrator: And she does. Now it is time to thresh the wheat. All the grain will make flour. The flour will make bread.

13

Little Red Hen: Who will help me thresh the wheat?

Dog: Not I! Are you joking?

Cat: Not I! You must be joking.

Mouse: Not I! That is so funny! It is really, really funny. But do tell me when it is time to nibble.

Goose: Not I! Ha ha! Hee hee! That is the funniest thing I have ever heard! Now go away and do not bother me.

Little Red Hen: Then I will do it myself.

Narrator: And she does.

Little Red Hen: Now it is time to go to the mill. I will grind the wheat into flour.

Narrator: She tries once more to get help.

Little Red Hen: Who will help me grind the wheat?

Dog: Not I! Ha Ha!

Cat: Not I! Ho Ho!

Mouse: Not I! Oh, you are a funny hen!

Goose: Not I! Your name should be "Silly Red Hen." Now go away and do not bother me.

Little Red Hen: Then I will do it myself.

Narrator: And she does.

Act 3

Narrator:	Little Red Hen does all the work. She plants the grain. She cuts the wheat. She threshes the grain. She grinds the flour.
Little Red Hen:	Oh, my. I am very tired now. But soon I will have bread. My chicks love bread!
Narrator:	One more time, she tries to get some help.
Little Red Hen:	Who will help me bake the bread?
Dog:	Not I!
Cat:	Not I!

Mouse: Not I! But is it time to nibble yet?

Goose: Not I! No, no, no, not I. Now go away and do not bother me. Honk!

Little Red Hen: All right. I do not need your help. I will bake it myself.

Narrator: And she does.

Song: Shortnin' Bread

Little Red Hen: Ah! My bread is ready.

Dog: Mmmm.

Cat: Mmmm.

Mouse: Yum! Yum! Yummy yum yum! I know it is time to nibble now.

Goose: Now that's what I call good eating. Bring me that bread!

Little Red Hen: Oh, really? I planted the grain. I cut the wheat. I threshed the grain. I ground the flour. I baked the bread. I did it all by myself.

Dog: So?

Cat: So?

Mouse: We know you are a hard worker.

Goose: Yes, yes, you are a hard worker. So what?

Little Red Hen: Yes, I did work hard. I have made good bread. There is plenty to eat. But who will help me eat this bread?

Dog: I will!

Cat: Me, too!

Mouse: Me, three! It is time to nibble at last.

Goose: Count me in, my fine friend!

Narrator: Little Red Hen smiles as wide as her beak can smile.

Little Red Hen: I am sure you want to eat the bread. But you did not help. You did not plant the grain. You did not cut the wheat. You did not thresh the grain. You did not grind the flour. You did not bake the bread.

Dog: What is your point?

Cat: Yes, what is your point?

Mouse: Hurry up! I'm hungry.

Goose: We are waiting to eat. You are bothering me!

Little Red Hen: Too bad for you. You did not help. Now you will not eat!

Narrator: Dog, Cat, Mouse, and Goose just stare at Little Red Hen. They lick their lips and bill. They smell the bread. But they can not eat it.

Little Red Hen: Come here, my little chicks! Mommy has made bread just for you and me.

Narrator: Little Red Hen and her chicks eat up all that good bread. And they do not need any help to do it.

I Had a Little Hen
Traditional

I had a little hen, the prettiest ever seen,
She washed up the dishes and kept the house clean.

She went to the mill to fetch us some flour,
And always got home in less than an hour.

She baked me my bread, she brewed me my ale,
She sat by the fire and told a fine tale!

 # Shortnin' Bread
Traditional

Put on the skillet, put on the lid,
Mama's gonna make a little shortnin' bread.
That ain't all she's gonna do,
Mama's gonna make a little coffee, too.

Chorus:
Mama's little baby loves shortnin', shortnin',
Mama's little baby loves shortnin' bread.
Mama's little baby loves shortnin', shortnin',
Mama's little baby loves shortnin' bread.

Three little children, lyin' in bed.
Two were sick and the other 'most dead.
Sent for the doctor and the doctor said,
"Give those children some shortnin' bread!"

Chorus

Glossary

ale—a type of drink

coop—a little house where chickens live

counts on—trusts; depends on

flour—a powder made from wheat that is used to bake bread, cake, and other food

grain—a small, hard seed

grind—to mash into small pieces or powder

lazy—not doing anything but lying around

mill—a building where wheat and other grains are ground into flour

nibble—a tiny bite; to take a tiny bite

shortnin' bread—a type of bread made in a frying pan, like cornbread

thresh—to separate the grain or seeds from a plant

zzzz—a sleeping noise, like snoring